Bumper Bii

Author – Dolly Stamer

This is a story about an early adventure that changed the outlook of a very young bird. This is a story about resilience and surviving in an unknown situation.

This story idea started with an actual observation of a live bird riding on the back bumper of a car. Why did I choose bluebirds? Some believe that the bluebird is a symbol of joy and hope.

Bluebirds can spot caterpillars and insects in tall grass at a remarkable distance of well over 50 yards. Bluebirds are very social and at times they gather in flocks over one hundred or more.

Bluebirds represent the very best in family life, as they defend nesting and feeding of their babies. That is why Bumper Bird was my choice as a bluebird.

by Dolly Stamer

by Dolly Stamer

Acknowledgements

First and foremost, I want to thank my husband, Mike, for encouraging my effort every step of the way in writing this book. He helped me to format the book, and he was my editor. I could not have asked for a more eloquent and brilliant editor and mentor. He believed in me and managed to help unfold my dream of this book into a reality.

Thank you to my son-in-law, Justin Miller, who worked diligently and artistically to illustrate the book cover. I am grateful that he was able to fit me into his busy schedule.

Thank you to my daughter, Jackie Miller, who after hearing the concept of my book, came up with the name for the "star of the show" Bumper Bird. She also was very kind and supportive toward the visions I had for this children's book.

I want to thank both of my wonderful granddaughters, Adella and Maia, who each have written and typed stories with me. These stories have created laughter and colored my life. The stories we wrote connected me to the inspiration that became Bumper Bird's Adventure.

Thank you to Kristina Tomasic, a young college student who developed some of the illustrations for this book.

I also want to thank my English Professor, David Jakolski PhD. He also suggested that I write more and encouraged me to take my writing seriously.

Bumper Bird's Adventure

by Dolly Stamer

Table of Contents

by Dolly Stamer

Bumper Bird's Adventure
by Dolly Stamer

Chapter 1 - The Story Begins

Once upon a time, high in a beautiful tree, in a very peaceful neighborhood, a mother bluebird sat nurturing her six beautiful eggs. She sat on these eggs and protected them until the day they all hatched.

1

by Dolly Stamer

All the flowers were perking up in the joy of springtime. All the grass stood firm and green and tall. All the clouds were floating in a sea of happiness due to the hatching of these six little birds.

Very soon the baby birds were chirping and looking around in their nest. At first, they saw their father bringing food to their mother. Their mother would feed the baby birds. Later, the birds saw their mother fly away to get food. She brought the food back and lovingly fed each of the baby birds.

The mother noticed each bluebird was becoming more alert and stronger day by day. From this, mother bird knew that this was the day that she would teach her babies their first flying lesson.

by Dolly Stamer

Chapter 2 – Flying Lessons

She encouraged them to fly for the very first time. She explained to them the important things to know about flying and knowing directions. She explained to them about flapping their wings without stopping. She taught them to be alert for unexpected conditions.

The time arrived to start their first practice. She said she would use a signal, which was two tweets to tell each bird in line it is their turn to fly. The babies were inspired. However, bluebird number six was the most reluctant.

At the signal, each bluebird took their turn for the first lesson.

Bluebird number one

JUMPED AND FRUMPED.

Bluebird number two

JUMPED AND LUMPED.

Bluebird number three

DIVED AND STRIVED.

Bluebird number four

DIVED AND SURVIVED.

Bluebird number five

DIVED AND FLIP-FLOPPED AND FLUTTERED TO THE GROUND.

Bluebird number six

DIVED AND THOUGHT – WHY ARE WE DOING THIS? WHY? SHE JUMPED AND DROPPED WITHOUT A SOUND TO THE GROUND.

by Dolly Stamer

Their mother saw that it was difficult for the baby birds on the first try. She knew this was normal. She talked to them once they reached the ground. She said that they will have to flap their wings even harder to get back up to the nest. She explained to them that they may need to find a lower branch first and then a higher branch. Then they will reach their nest.

The second day for flying lessons arrived. Again, mother bluebird told her babies that it is time for the next flying practice. She used the same two tweet signal, so that each bird would fly one at a time. She wanted to watch each bird to see how well they did. Once again, all the babies were inspired. However, bluebird number six was the most inspired.

Each bluebird once again took their turn.

Bluebird number one
GLIDED AND SLIDED.
Bluebird number two
FLEW GRACEFULLY DOWN.
Bluebird number three
TRIED AND STRIVED.
Bluebird number four
DIVED AND LANDED SMOOTHLY.
Bluebird number five
FLEW OUT AND DOWN.
Bluebird number six
DIVED AND SWOOPED DOWN QUICKEST OF ALL.

The little birdies had more confidence to fly upward and back into the tree after the second lesson. They listened to their mother talk about how to improve their flying skills. She wanted them to know how to decide which direction to fly. This would help them wherever they happen to be.

On the third day, all the birds had an even greater feeling of confidence about flying. They were up early and out of the nest, sitting excitedly on a nearby branch. They were ready to attempt their third lesson. This would involve being able to fly in various directions.

   It is still early in the morning. Bluebird number six looked up at the sky. It was a pale pink, and a pale yellow with various shades of blue. She cheerfully looked forward to the next flying lesson. She thought that this would be an exciting and useful adventure.

Bluebird number six saw the branches of the tree where she was sitting. They were lovely, tall and leafy green branches. What a radiantly beautiful sight to her young eyes. She began to daydream.

She imagined herself in the grass playing with her brothers and sisters. This was the usual reward for a lesson well learned. She recalled the white sidewalk leading up to a yellow house with a red door. She wondered who might live inside that house.

Then she was suddenly interrupted from her daydream by her mother calling the birds to start their next lesson. Her mother tweeted her two tweets to each of the baby bluebirds.

Especially this time, all the babies were inspired. However, bluebird number six was the most inspired and extremely anxious to begin.

Each bird took their turn for the third lesson.

Bluebird number one
SOARED WITH SPEED TO THE NEAREST TREE.
Bluebird number two
JUMPED WITH HASTE AND NO WASTE.
Bluebird number three
LEAPED AND WAS FREE TO FLY.
Bluebird number four
DIVED AND ENDURED.
Bluebird number five
FLEW UP AND FLIP-FLOPPED FROM THE VERY TIP TOP.
Bluebird number six

FLEW OUT IN A SWIRL. SHE BECAME DIZZY AND FELL AND FELL AND ALMOST FELL INTO THE WELL. BUT HERE IS WHAT HAPPENED NEXT.

Chapter 3 – What Happened Next

It just so happened that a car was parked near the yellow house with the red door. She luckily recovered from her tumble and glided safely onto the bumper of the car.

by Dolly Stamer

A man got into the car and started the engine. Oh, how frightening. The car started moving without wings.

The man drove away with her on the bumper. She saw that she was getting further away from the tree. She saw her mother in the grass playing with her brothers and sisters. The yellow house with the red door and the white sidewalk were getting smaller and smaller. They would soon fade out of sight.

From this event, bluebird number six earned the nickname of Bumper Bird. Little Bumper Bird, while still clinging to the bumper of the car, started feeling a sense of freedom. Yet she also felt a sense of fear as the yellow house faded away. Not even the picket fence was in sight.

She no longer knew where she was. These new places were foreign to her. She started wondering how she would get back home. She thought "OK, take a deep breath and everything will get better. Here goes - Inhale. Deep breath and everything will get better".

She took another deep breath. Now she understood why her mother wanted to teach them how to recognize landmarks, trees, houses, and other details of their surroundings. Her mother wanted them to know how to decide which direction to fly. Now she knew why they did all those lessons. She realized for the first time how important those lessons were.

How will she ever learn her sense of direction? How will she ever make her mother proud of her? How will she ever again play with her brothers and sisters? These thoughts made her feel sad. She fought the tears from her little birdie eyes and kept them very wide open, even though it was very scary.

The car moved faster. Bumper bird had no idea where she was. When the car slowed down, this made her wobble and slide around. However, she was still clinging desperately to the bumper.

Chapter 4 - The Food Market

The car pulled right in front of a food market and stopped. She wanted to fly away, but she could not. The reason is that she did not learn her sense of direction yet. So, she had no choice but to hang onto the bumper for dear life!

by Dolly Stamer

The man got out of the car and walked toward the food market. But then the man heard a tiny tweet, tweet. He turned around to see what it was. Bumper Bird knew about holding still and being quiet. The man looked backward, forward, and all around. He shrugged his shoulders and thought he imagined the tweet, tweet. He went into the store and picked up a delivery of packages and returned to the car.

Bumper Bird was afraid she would never return home to her mother and brothers and sisters and the happy little neighborhood that she had learned to love in her little birdie life. The man started the engine again and drove away with her still clinging to the bumper.

Little by little she started recognizing the yellow house on the corner. She recognized and was very comfortable with the white sidewalk going to the red door of the yellow house with the picket fence.

This time, all the flowers were really perked up in the joy of springtime. All the grass stood firmer and greener and taller like confident soldiers.

Best of all, she saw their majestic tree and she saw all the baby bluebirds gathered around mother bluebird as they played. She really loved playing with her feathered family. Finally, the car came to a stop near the same place where the adventure began. The clouds were really floating in a sea of happiness because Bumper Bird was home at last.

For the first time in her little bluebird life, she realized that there is no place like home. She was able to jump off the bumper in front of her mother and all her brothers and sisters.

Mother bird, with a tear in her eye, greeted Bumper Bird. The baby brothers and sisters gathered around.

Mother and father bluebird tweeted back and forth to each other and decided before sunset that evening to take all the babies on a learning tour through the neighborhood. Father bluebird was determined to first demonstrate to the young birds the flying skills he had learned throughout his life.

Chapter 5 – More to Learn

Through his soaring demonstration, he showed how to gain altitude and make use of the wind currents in the air above. As he was gliding, he used the position of his wings to deflect the air downward. This kept him steady, soaring swiftly and straight with little effort. All the young birds could not wait to try this.

The mother planned to teach them how to recognize landmarks, trees, houses and other details of their surroundings. Mother bird wanted them to know how to decide which direction to fly to safety.

Mother bird called to Father bird to lead in these lessons. She explained her plan to have everyone fly together. She had in mind several lessons they would learn as they went along on their trip.

They started with a small step of flying to the end of the yard and looking back at the tree and surrounding area. She wanted them to notice how things looked from further away. Then they flew back.

She explained to them that they would then fly a longer distance beyond the end of the yard and down the street. With each of these flights, they began to soar higher and smoother as she would explain what the babies should notice and what they should learn.

Finally, they flew and soared around their entire neighborhood. They were able to notice different houses, different trees, different objects. This helped them to see when they were returning home to their tree.

by Dolly Stamer

20

They all circled the neighborhood and truly felt secure listening to all the teaching chirps from mother and father bluebird.

Bumper bird felt like this was certainly a very good lesson as did her brothers and sisters. The family was so excited at being together and returning home.

This prompted Bumper Bird to explain each of the events during her unplanned adventure. The entire family looked to Bumper Bird with admiration.

Each bird looked directly at Bumper Bird and tweeted their joyful reply. Bumper Bird, you are wonderful. Bumper Bird, you have strength. Bumper Bird, you held on tight through your first adventure in life. Bumper Bird, you have stamina. Bumper Bird, you have endurance and determination. Bumper Bird, you are courageous.

Bumper Bird heard all of this. She enjoyed their encouraging chirps. She did not fully understand all their praises and compliments. But somehow, she knew this was a very important step in her life. She was glad to be home. Now she knew why she needed to learn all the lessons that her mother and father taught!

Bumper Bird realized this adventure had helped her to grow in wisdom and understanding. She wondered about a time in the future when she could soar up high into the sky and explore another new horizon. She thought what a wonderful adventure that could be. However, for now, she would enjoy the beauty of her surroundings and the comfort and happiness of her family.

THE END

by Dolly Stamer

About the Author

Dolly Stamer is a new and enthusiastic author. After working full time for over 36 years, she decided to combine her years of accumulated college credits and return to college in order to earn an Associate Degree. She completed her Associate Degree in the year 2020. Because of the Pandemic she was able to celebrate graduation in 2021. She was influenced strongly in English 101 by English Professor, David Jakolski PhD. He also suggested that she write more and encouraged her to do so.

This sparked an interest in writing stories by herself, as well as with her granddaughters. Each grandchild contributed greatly to her interest in children's story writing.

Bumper Bird's Adventure

Her granddaughter, Maia, was a great inspiration as the first to put the story about Bumper Bird into a total neighborhood scene.

by Dolly Stamer

Dolly's interest in birds has prompted her to write her first children's story about these humorous, daring bluebirds.

She had been known by friends and neighbors as someone who loves parakeets. As a result, friends occasionally rescued birds from neighborhood swimming pools and nearby trees and brought them to her.

In her home, the parakeets raised several clutches of baby parakeets. These parakeets were very colorful birds and were mostly given away. Dolly has owned parakeets since her childhood.

Bumper Bird's Adventure

Here are pictures of a clutch of Parakeets that Dolly raised from birth. They were lovingly cared for and very playful. They were wonderfully tame and got along well.

by Dolly Stamer

Printed in Great Britain
by Amazon

37493470R00023